Katie Woo

Piggy Bank Problems

by Fran Manushkin

illustrated by Tammie Lyon

Katie Woo is published by Picture Window Books,
1710 Roe Crest Drive
North Mankato, Minnesota 56003
www.capstonepub.com

Text © 2013 Fran Manushkin
Illustrations © 2013 Picture Window Books

Library of Congress Cataloging-in-Publication Data
Manushkin, Fran.
 Piggy bank problems / by Fran Manushkin; illustrated by Tammie Lyon.
      p. cm. — (Katie Woo)
 Summary: Katie goes to the bank with her friends JoJo and Pedro, and learns the value of having a place to keep her money.
 ISBN 978-1-4048-7654-5 (library binding)
 ISBN 978-1-4048-8048-1 (pbk.)
 1. Woo, Katie (Fictitious character)—Juvenile fiction. 2. Chinese Americans—Juvenile fiction. 3. Banks and banking—Juvenile fiction. 4. Piggy banks—Juvenile fiction. 5. Money—Juvenile fiction. [1. Chinese Americans—Fiction. 2. Banks and banking—Fiction. 3. Piggy banks—Fiction. 4. Money—Fiction.] I. Lyon, Tammie, ill. II. Title. III. Series: Manushkin, Fran. Katie Woo.
 PZ7.M3195Pig 2013
 813.54—dc23   2012029148

Art Director: Kay Fraser
Graphic Designer: Kristi Carlson

Photo Credits:
Greg Holch, pg. 26
Tammie Lyon, pg. 26

Printed in the United States of America in Stevens Point, Wisconsin.

009919R

Table of Contents

Chapter 1
Jingle, Jingle

JoJo and Katie both had piggy banks.

"My bank is full," said JoJo. "Hear it jingle?"

"Yes!" said Katie. "I love that sound."

"I'm bringing my money to the bank," JoJo said. "They will keep it safe."

"I'll come too," Katie decided. "I've never been to a bank."

Katie and JoJo jingled their piggy banks as they walked along.

"It's such a happy sound." Katie smiled.

"Maybe Pedro wants to come too," said Katie. Pedro did!

He told Katie, "I'll show you how to give the bank your money."

"I don't know," said Katie. "I like my piggy bank."

Pedro told Katie, "I'm saving my money to buy a little helicopter. It can really fly!"

"That sounds great!" said Katie.

"I'm saving my money
for a guitar," said JoJo. "I
can make up songs and play
them for you."

"That sounds cool," said
Katie.

Chapter 2
At the Bank

Soon they reached the

bank. "Where are the piles of

money?" asked Katie.

"In the safe," said her dad.

"Can I take some?" asked

Katie.

"No way!" he said.

JoJo took the money out of her piggy bank. Katie helped her count it.

"Your bank is empty now," Katie sighed. "No jingle."

JoJo gave her money to

the bank teller.

"My money is safe here,"

she told Katie. "I cannot lose

it."

"Yesterday, I lost a
quarter," said Katie sadly. "It
fell out of a hole in
my pocket."

"It's more fun to find money," said Pedro. "Last week, I found a dollar on the sidewalk."

"Lucky you!" said Katie.

"Would you like to put
your money in the bank?"
asked Katie's dad.

"No," insisted Katie. "I'm
keeping my money in my
piggy bank."

Chapter 3

Crash!

Just then, Miss Winkle

came into the bank.

"Everybody comes here,"

Katie said. "This bank is

very popular!"

The bank teller gave Miss
Winkle some money. But
as she started to leave, she
dropped a ten-dollar bill.

Katie ran to pick it up.

"Watch out!" warned
Pedro. Too late!

Katie tripped, and her
piggy bank went flying.
CRASH! It broke!

Money rolled everywhere!

"Don't worry!" said Pedro.

"We will help pick it up!"

"Let's see who can find

the most money!" said JoJo.

Miss Winkle won!

Katie made piles of pennies

and nickels and dimes and

quarters.

"I'm rich!" said Katie. "But

where will I put my money?

My piggy bank is in pieces."

"There's plenty of room in this bank," said JoJo.

"Okay," agreed Katie. "I will keep it here."

"That's a good idea," said Pedro. "But I'm sorry you broke your bank."

"Don't worry!" Katie smiled. "I'm using some of my money to buy a new piggy bank. Then I can keep jingling my money."

Katie and her dad went to the store. He gave Katie four quarters to put in her new bank.

Katie jingled it all the way home.

About the Author

Fran Manushkin is the author of many popular picture books, including *Baby, Come Out!*; *Latkes and Applesauce: A Hanukkah Story*; *The Tushy Book*; *The Belly Book*; and *Big Girl Panties*. There is a real Katie Woo — she's Fran's great-niece — but she never gets in half the trouble of the Katie Woo in the books. Fran writes on her beloved Mac computer in New York City, without the help of her two naughty cats, Chaim and Goldy.

About the Illustrator

Tammie Lyon began her love for drawing at a young age while sitting at the kitchen table with her dad. She continued her love of art and eventually attended the Columbus College of Art and Design, where she earned a bachelors degree in fine art. After a brief career as a professional ballet dancer, she decided to devote herself full time to illustration. Today she lives with her husband, Lee, in Cincinnati, Ohio. Her dogs, Gus and Dudley, keep her company as she works in her studio.

Glossary

empty (EMP-tee)—containing nothing

insisted (in-SIS-ted)—demanding something firmly

jingle (JING-guhl)—a tinkling or ringing sound made by the movement of small bells, keys, or coins

popular (POP-yuh-lur)—liked or enjoyed by many people

sighed (SYED)—breathed out deeply, often to express sadness or relief

Discussion Questions

1. Katie loves the sound of her coins jingling. What sounds do you enjoy?

2. Have you ever been to a bank? Describe what a bank is like.

3. Pedro was saving up for a helicopter, and JoJo was saving up for a guitar. Have you ever saved up for something? What?

Writing Prompts

1. Writers often describe things to help the readers get a picture in their minds. Write two or three sentences to describe Katie's first piggy bank.

2. What are some ways that you could make money? Write a list of three ideas.

3. Write about a time that you broke something. What was it, how did it happen, and how did you feel?

Make Your Own Piggy Bank!

With this project, you can turn a 2-liter soda bottle into a piggy bank. Your money might not jingle in it, but it will still make a nice sound!

What you need:

- paintbrush
- paint bowl
- pink acrylic paint
- 2 toilet paper tubes
- scissors
- clean 2-liter plastic bottle
- 2 googly eyes, 5/8 inch wide
- pink, two-holed button, 3/4 inch wide
- craft glue
- craft knife
- pink pipe cleaner

What you do:

1. Paint the outside of the tubes pink. Paint half of the inside of one tube pink. Let dry.

2. Paint the bottle and bottle cap pink. Let dry. Repeat if the first coat is not thick enough.

3. Make the ears by cutting two U shapes out of the tube that is painted pink inside. Cut three 1/4 inch slits at the bottom of each ear. Fold these flaps back. These will be gluing tabs for the ears.

4. Make the legs by cutting four 1½ -inch-long sections from the tubes. Trim each leg to fit the shape of the bottle.

5. Attach the legs, ears, and eyes with the craft glue. Attach the pink button onto the bottle cap with the glue, too. Let dry.

6. Ask a grown-up to cut a rectangular coin slot in the pig's back, using a craft knife.

7. Wind the pipe cleaner around a finger to make a curly tail. Glue it on the back.

THE FUN DOESN'T STOP HERE!

Discover more at www.capstonekids.com

♥ Videos & Contests

✿ Games & Puzzles

♥ Friends & Favorites

✿ Authors & Illustrators

Find cool websites and more books like this one at www.facthound.com. Just type in the Book ID: 9781404876545 and you're ready to go!